THE UNDERPANTS ZOO

W9-AHJ-459

TO ELIZABETH

No part of this publication may be reproduced, stored in a retrieval system, or transmitted in any form or by any means, electronic, mechanical, photocopying, recording, or otherwise, without written permission of the publisher. For information regarding permission, write to Orchard Books, Scholastic Inc., Attention: Permissions Department, 557 Broadway, New York, NY 10012.

ISBN 978-0-545-45396-7

Text and illustrations copyright © 2011 by Brian Sendelbach.
All rights reserved. Published by Orchard Books, an imprint of Scholastic Inc. ORCHARD BOOKS and design are registered trademarks of Watts Publishing Group, Ltd., used under license. SCHOLASTIC and associated logos are trademarks and/or registered trademarks of Scholastic Inc.

12 11 10 9 8 7 6 5 4 3 2 1   12 13 14 15 16 17/0

Printed in the U.S.A.   40

First Scholastic paperback printing, March 2012

The display type was set in Circus Mouse.
The text was set in Linotype Conrad.
The art was created using acrylic paints.
Book design by Whitney Lyle

THE UNDERPANTS ZOO

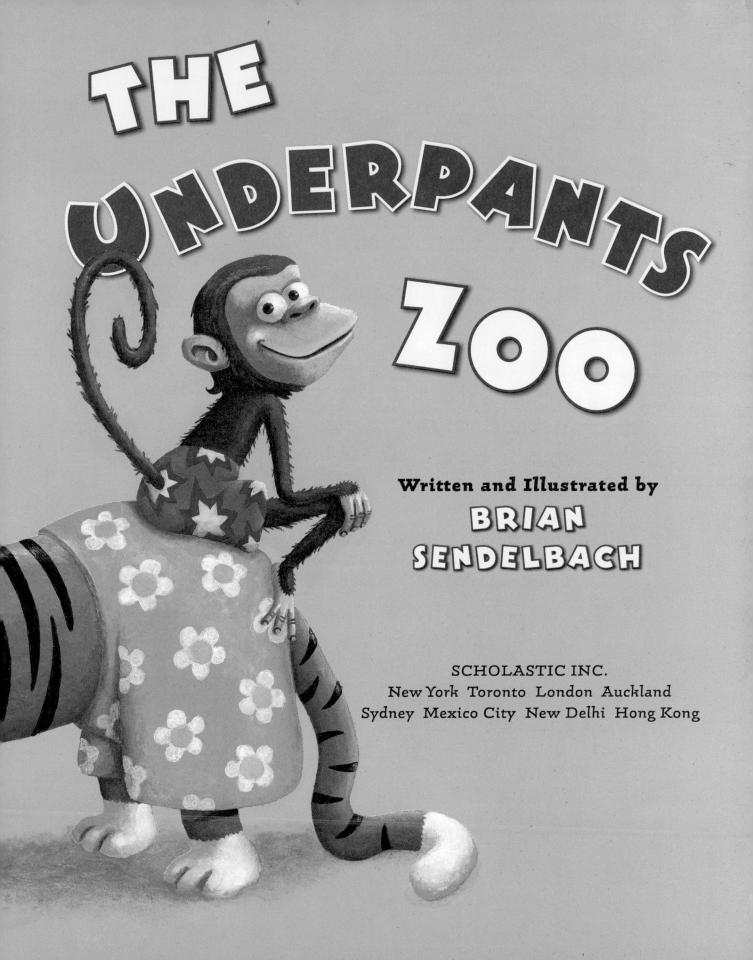

Written and Illustrated by
BRIAN SENDELBACH

SCHOLASTIC INC.
New York Toronto London Auckland
Sydney Mexico City New Delhi Hong Kong

There's a new zoo in town,
and here's what I've heard —
**THE
UNDERPANTS
ZOO**
is completely absurd. . . .

Come in and find out
why there's been such a fuss.
It's a zoo where the animals
wear underpants . . . just like us!

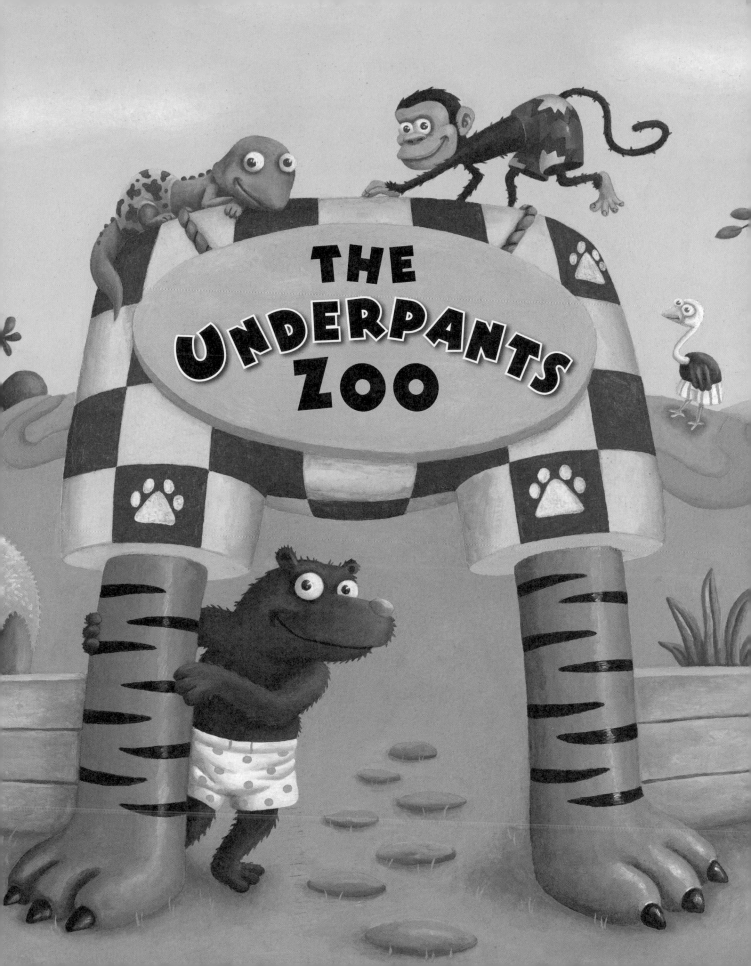

THE UNDERPANTS ZOO

It's important for **LION'S**
to appear royal and grand.

CAMEL says, "Mine keep getting filled up with sand!"

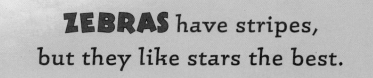

ZEBRAS have stripes,
but they like stars the best.

LEOPARD prefers spots,
as you may have guessed.

HIPPO'S have hearts,
because she's such a romantic.

ELEPHANT'S size is
Extra-Jumbo Gigantic.

KANGAROO'S boxers
need plenty of bounce.

For the sleepy SLOTHS,
it's comfort that counts.

The **SNAKES** are good friends,
so they share the same pair.

Make fun of **CROCODILE'S** style . . .
if you dare!

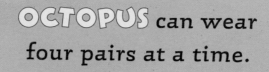

OCTOPUS can wear
four pairs at a time.

DOLPHINS in long johns?
It boggles the mind!

The **PENGUINS** chill their
underpants in the freezer....

The MONKEYS' wild trunks
are always crowd-pleasers!

It may look as though **ANTEATER**
is doing some silly dance,
but look closely and you'll see —
HIS UNDERPANTS HAVE GOT ANTS!

The Underpants Zoo
(I am sorry to say)
is closing its gates
for the rest of the day.

But we'll visit again!
We'll drop by very soon.
Next time we'll stay
for the whole afternoon.

THE UNDERPANTS ZOO

CLOSED FOR UNDERPANTS DE-ANTSING